anythink

Erin and Her New Pet

The Sound of Short E

by Joanne Meier and Cecilia Minden • illustrated by Bob Ostrom

The Child's World

Published by The Child's World®
1980 Lookout Drive
Mankato, MN 56003-1705
800-599-READ
www.childsworld.com

The Child's World®: Mary Berendes, Publishing Director
The Design Lab: Design and page production

Library of Congress Cataloging-in-Publication Data
Meier, Joanne D.
 Erin and her new pet : the sound of short e / by Joanne
Meier and Cecilia Minden illustrated by Bob Ostrom.
    p. cm.
 ISBN 978-1-60253-398-1 (library bound : alk. paper)
 1. English language—Vowels—Juvenile literature.
 2. English language—Phonetics—Juvenile literature
 3. Reading—Phonetic method—Juvenile literature.
 I. Minden, Cecilia. II. Ostrom, Bob. III. Title.
 PE1157.M544 2010
 [E]—dc22   2010002912

Printed in the United States of America in Mankato, MN.
July 2010
F11538

NOTE TO PARENTS AND EDUCATORS:

The Child's World® has created this series with the goal of exposing children to engaging stories and illustrations that assist in phonics development. The books in the series will help children learn the relationships between the letters of written language and the individual sounds of spoken language. This contact helps children learn to use these relationships to read and write words.

The books in this series follow a similar format. An introductory page, to be read by an adult, introduces the child to the phonics feature, or sound, that will be highlighted in the book. Read this page to the child, stressing the phonic feature. Help the student learn how to form the sound with her mouth. The story and engaging illustrations follow the introduction. At the end of the story, word lists categorize the feature words into their phonic elements.

Each book in this series has been carefully written to meet specific readability requirements. Close attention has been paid to elements such as word count, sentence length, and vocabulary. Readability formulas measure the ease with which the text can be read and understood. Each book in this series has been analyzed using the Spache readability formula.

Reading research suggests that systematic phonics instruction can greatly improve students' word recognition, spelling, and comprehension skills. This series assists in the teaching of phonics by providing students with important opportunities to apply their knowledge of phonics as they read words, sentences, and text.

The letter e makes two sounds.

The long sound of **e** sounds like **e** as in: *bee* and *peek.*

The short sound of **e** sounds like **e** as in: *egg* and *hen.*

In this book, you will read words that have the short **e** sound as in: *pet, bell, red,* and *nest.*

Erin has a new pet.

Her name is Penny.

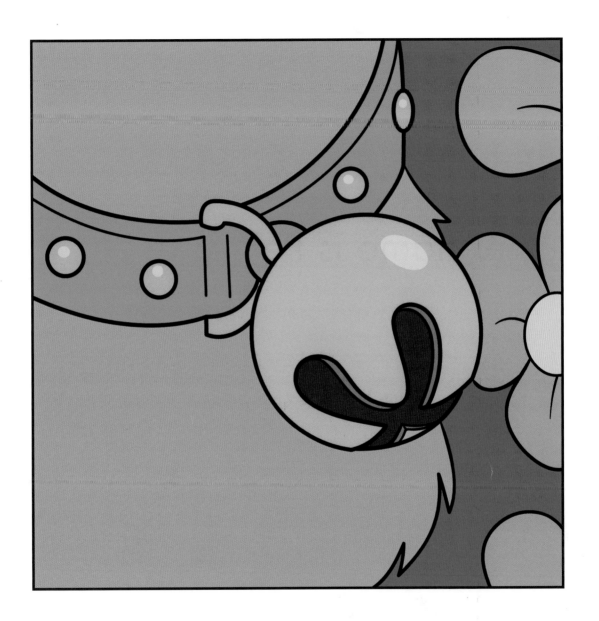

Erin and Penny like to walk.

They hear a little bell.

Here comes Ember. Ember is a cat. Ember has a bell around her neck.

Erin and Penny walk some more. They hear a bird singing.

A red bird is in a nest.

What a nice song!

Erin and Penny walk some more. They hear a girl calling. It is Erin's friend, Ellie.

"Hello, Ellie. This is my

new pet."

"What a nice puppy," says Ellie. "What is her name?"

"Her name is Penny," says Erin.

Erin and Penny walk some more. "We are home, Penny." Penny gives Erin a big, wet puppy kiss.

Fun Facts

Some bells may be small enough to fit on your pet's collar, but not the Liberty Bell in Philadelphia, Pennsylvania! This bell was built in 1751 in London, England, and was later shipped to the United States. It weighs 2,080 pounds (943 kilograms) and is 3 feet (1 meter) tall. The Liberty Bell is a symbol of U.S. freedom.

More pets live in the United States than people! Americans own more than 77 million cats, about 65 million dogs, and countless other pets such as fish and hamsters. Many historians believe that dogs were the first animals to be kept as pets in ancient times. In ancient Egypt, cat owners used their pets to hunt birds and other small animals.

Activity

Marching in a Pet Parade

Your town may host parades on holidays, but some communities also organize annual parades in which owners can march with their pets. Check with your local community center or the mayor's office to see if your town has a yearly pet parade. If it does, consider how well behaved your pet is. It will have to get along with other animals to be part of the parade. If you decide to participate, make sure your parents bring a camera and take pictures of you and your pet as you march!

To Learn More

Books

About the Sound of Short E

Moncure, Jane Belk. *My "e" Sound Box®*. Mankato, MN: The Child's World, 2009.

Metz, Lynn. *Every Egg: Learning the Short E Sound*. New York: PowerKids Press, 2002.

About Bells

Berger, Samantha, and Rick Brown (illustrator). *Please Don't Tell About Mom's Bell*. New York: Scholastic, 2002.

Jango-Cohen, Judith. *The Liberty Bell*. Minneapolis, MN: Lerner Publications, 2004.

About Pets

Driscoll, Laura, and Christian Slade (illustrator). *Presidential Pets*. New York: Grosset & Dunlap, 2009.

Javernick, Ellen, and Kevin O'Malley (illustrator). *The Birthday Pet*. New York: Marshall Cavendish Children, 2009.

Palatini, Margie, and Bruce Whately (illustrator). *The Perfect Pet*. New York: HarperCollins Publishers, 2003.

Web Sites

Visit our home page for lots of links about the Sound of Short E:

childsworld.com/links

Note to Parents, Teachers, and Librarians: We routinely check our Web links to make sure they're safe, active sites—so encourage your readers to check them out!

Short E
Feature Words

Proper Names

Ellie

Ember

Erin

Penny

Feature Words in Medial Position

bell

hello

neck

nest

pet

red

wet

About the Authors

Joanne Meier, PhD, has worked as an elementary school teacher, university professor, and researcher. She earned her BA in early childhood education from the University of South Carolina, and her MEd and PhD in education from the University of Virginia. She currently works as a literacy consultant for schools and private organizations. Joanne lives in Virginia with her husband Eric, daughters Kella and Erin, two cats, and a gerbil.

Cecilia Minden, PhD, is the former director of the Language and Literacy Program at the Harvard Graduate School of Education. She is now a reading consultant for school and library publications. She earned her PhD in reading education from the University of Virginia. Cecilia and her husband, Dave Cupp, live outside Chapel Hill, North Carolina. They enjoy sharing their love of reading with their grandchildren, Chelsea and Qadir.

About the Illustrator

Bob Ostrom has been illustrating children's books for nearly twenty years. A graduate of the New England School of Art & Design at Suffolk University, Bob has worked for such companies as Disney, Nickelodeon, and Cartoon Network. He lives in North Carolina with his wife Melissa and three children, Will, Charlie, and Mae.